The ZOMBIE'S Survival Guide

Thrive In The Zombie Apocalypse
After You Turn...

By HET MADDEN

From A ZOMBIE'S Perspective

Calvin A. L. Miller II
Artwork By Alan R. Gandy

ISBN- 0615404960
EAN13- 9780615404967

Published in 2010 by Zilyon Publishing, Inc.

Zilyon Publishing, Inc.
4094 Fountainside Lane
Fairfax, VA 22030
www.ZilyonPublishing.com
www.CalvinALMillerII.com
cal_in_space@yahoo.com

By Calvin A. L. Miller II
Artwork By Alan R. Gandy
Edited By Etienne DeForest and Philip Moortgat

THERE ARE A ZILYON STORIES TO TELL...WHAT'S YOURS

Love Bites. Hate Eats...

The ZOMBIE'S Survival Guide

Thrive In The Zombie Apocalypse *After You Turn...*

The "Zombie" Apocalypse is coming. It's not "if" it's "when", and if you think you are going to be one of the brave survivors you see in the movies and video games or read about in books and graphic novels you are sadly mistaken. You know who I mean, the handsome and tough hero who was a Navy Seal that women love and men want to be. Or the beautiful, big breasted, brilliant heroine with a PhD in "Science". You aren't even the wisecracking sidekick who lives to defend the heroes. You are a regular person, an everyman. Just as I was before I wrote this book... So face it, the odds are much more in favor of you becoming one of the Undead. A Ghoul. A Dead. A "Zombie".

But don't worry, there is hope. There are ways for you to "live" a very happy and rewarding "life" after you turn. How long, well that depends. But you might as well enjoy virtual immortality while you can. Sure, it's not as cool as being a vampire. They get the late nights partying, looking like the heroes I mentioned above, the cool clothes, and getting to sleep all day. No, you will be a staggering, oozing, puss-filled mess. Think of it as having the flu times a million.

But how can you fight Healthies armed with weapons that can be anything from a boy with a screwdriver to a soldier with an automatic rifle? And what about fire, armored vehicles, and explosives? You will not only have physical limitations but you will also be stupid, right?

Wrong.

Many "zombies" retain much of their intelligence after they turn. And many find ways to gain even more, as I did. The ones that are out in the open and shuffling toward people who have guns or other weapons are the dumb ones. The ones that weren't prepared. The smart ones know what to do. They go unnoticed. They wait for their chance to attack. They plot. But if the "Zombie Apocalypse" is coming and hasn't happened yet, how do I know all of this?

Because it has already started.

It just hasn't reached you yet, or maybe you're not aware. The mind can play tricks.

And because I'm Hetfield Madden.

And I'm a "Zombie"...

The Undead. What You Will Become...

The Undead

So you don't want to die. Nobody *really* does, but it's been a big part of life since the earth cooled and during a "zombie" apocalypse it's even bigger, or smaller in some ways. Deads (this is my word for "zombies", a word I find insulting, but I will use it in this Guide when necessary) will outnumber you, if they already don't, and you will get bitten, die, and turn. You will reanimate and get up and walk. You will remember things, how much who knows, but you will be undead. Not dead, but not alive. Now the verdict is still out on whether you turn simply by dying, and not just by being bitten by a Dead. I believe you do, because I have seen Deads that are completely unmarked; no bites, no nothing, walking around. Could they have been infected some other way? Blood transfusion or food maybe? And then died and come back? Perhaps, but I doubt it. Many theories exist, including that the disease is airborne but only infects the subject after death, or the airborne virus infects you while you are alive but doesn't kill you. It waits until you die to reanimate you. No matter. You die, you come back. It doesn't get any simpler. Even slow Deads will turn you. One bites one, who bites another and so on.

Being newly undead, you are going to need to know how to survive. Some of you reading this book may already be a Dead. You may or may not realize it yet. This is one of the problems with being undead. Realization is cloudy and perception is usually skewed. You may even think your life is the same as it has always been. The mind of the recently deceased plays tricks and memories and dreams cloud reality. Soon enough the real world will seep in and replace any delusions that you are still living your "normal" life.

If you want to know the truth take your temperature if you are able.

If you are undead it will be the same as room temperature, roughly. Feeling for a pulse or heartbeat is misleading as the heart is a muscle and in many cases still beats, although the blood it pumps is as dead as the Dead whose chest it beats in.

I know you've probably read that the hearts of the Undead do not beat, but I assure you this is not true. As long as the heart is safely tucked away inside the chest it will function as well as, if not better than, a Healthy's. Both voluntary and involuntary muscles continue to function, whether needed or not.

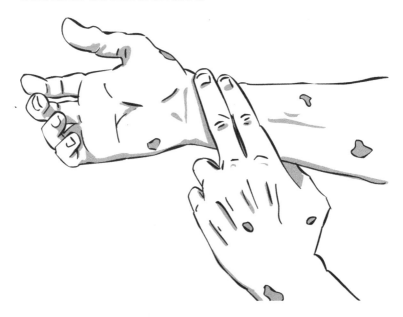

Feeling For A Pulse.

In any event, please continue reading. It WILL get easier the more you read. The information in this Guide is invaluable and will help you remain "alive" to fight the Healthies (this is a word used for the uninfected population who don't give a damn about you and want you eliminated) and make them pay. Well, there it is I guess. My ulterior motive... An educated Dead is a strong ally. The Healthies are responsible for the Wrath virus that caused all this (More on Wrath in later, slightly uncomfortable chapters) and what do we get in return? Shot at, herded into internment camps, and "studied"! Like animals!

I was in an Infected Containment Center and have the forehead brand to prove it. Once it all started to hit the fan the Government wasted no time in herding us away and trying to protect the "innocent".

Well I, for one, know there are no innocents. Anywhere.

We are experimented on, tortured, and cut up like cattle to see both how the infection spreads and the best way to kill it.

And the best way to kill us.

Subject Inside A Containment Center

So read this book, commit it to memory, and take it to the Healthies. If your undead comrades aren't able to do what's in this Guide, help them to learn. There are numerous guides that show Healthies how to survive us... How to eliminate our "plague" on them, what weapons to use to kill us, and the best and easiest way to do it. As if we were animals. This Guide is for us and shows how to survive, thrive, and eliminate, them.

Is This Going To Hurt? What To Expect, From Being Bitten To Your First Kill.

In short, yes it *is* going to hurt, and like hell. Dying hurts, a lot. Both physically and emotionally. You will feel more pain than you have ever felt. Pain that causes some to throw themselves off buildings or into oncoming traffic. But the pain can be soothed by feeding on Healthies. Raw meat from any mammal will work, in fact, but the effects are much more temporary with animal meat.

Raw Meat

You need to feed on Healthies. And don't worry, if you feed on a fellow Dead accidentally (or on purpose) it will not kill you. In fact it will happen. Frenzy is a phenomenon that occurs under the right conditions when enough hungry Deads are in a confined space. Much like when locusts swarm, only we attack each other until something stops us or we just stop. This will be covered more in a later part of this Guide.

But back to the pain...

At first you will feel like you have the flu. Or a cold. You will feel the need to rest, and the desire to be alone. As you begin to feel more and more ill, you will begin to vomit profusely and experience an intestinal nausea like you have never felt as you completely soil yourself. You will also run a very high fever, usually above 105 degrees.

Symptom Of Infection. Vomiting.

Some feel the moment they die, some don't, but we all know the moment we turn. It's a mix of fear and euphoria. The fear of death and the euphoria of being free from the chains of life. Almost immediately hunger will burn inside you. You will try and eat "normal" food, but will throw it right back up. This will be confusing, but soon you'll realize what you truly crave. Then you'll find yourself around what you truly need... A Healthy.

At first, you'll feel nothing, really. You will simply see a person standing there. You will have smelled him and felt a strange longing or hunger. You'll walk up to him, and he will most likely be horrified by the site of you. A word of warning, be careful approaching Healthies. Most are at least partially dangerous, especially those that are out among the population during the time of apocalypse.

Cricket Bat Wielding Healthy

They will be ready for a fight once the apocalypse has fully engaged, and will be looking to remove us and all of our ilk from the face of the earth.

You know this because you either are or you were a Healthy. Most likely if you approach from the front you will be beaten with a blunt object or shot between the eyes. Normally you would expect help from your fellow man, but they do not help us once we turn. They kill us. When you get close enough to a Healthy, however you manage this, the urge will come over you quickly. You will attack and feed uncontrollably, like your body is being guided by a force other than your own. You will ravenously attack and kill a human being, eating the cadaver before or after it dies. And any pain you felt before will be gone.

Covered in flesh and blood from your kill you most likely will not be able to stop until you are full or the corpse is fully eaten.

This will disturb you emotionally, but you can't give in to these feelings. This is now your nature. Any religious views you have will come into the mix as well.

"How could God do this to us, to me?" you may think. Well he did, it was easy, and you have to get used to it. You will most likely devolve into a Class C Dead (more on Classes later), a typical "zombie" type, so quickly it will be a struggle to think and reason. You will know you are having trouble too. You will feel less than you were and be angry you have to struggle to understand the environment around you. But you must soldier on and embrace what you have become. Trying to understand why this happened will only hold you back from realizing your full potential. Why does the wind blow? Why does the earth turn? They just do. Accept and embrace.

Soon after you turn you may experience several... repercussions... of death. Some of us experience rigor mortis, especially those who turn and do not keep moving.

Moving keeps the dying tissue limber and the joints and muscles free from locking and stiffening.

Stiffened, Rigor Mortis Laden Arm

If you don't bleed out from wounds received before or after you turn, blood will pool inside your body and this will be governed by gravity. Stand upright and it will pool in your legs. Lie down, it will pool towards the ground. The best way to fix this is to slice a hole in the area of the blood pooling to release it.

The pain from the pooling blood can range from none at all to a cold burning sensation that is nearly unbearable and only assuaged by getting all of the offending blood removed at once.

When cutting to create an escape for the painful and now completely useless fluid, you must be careful not to slice through muscle or tendons. Because you no longer heal, any damage you do will be permanent and will severely limit your mobility. You are dead, remember? If you can take the pooling, it's best to just leave it alone. You will invariably be wounded in the near future and the blood will come out sooner or later.

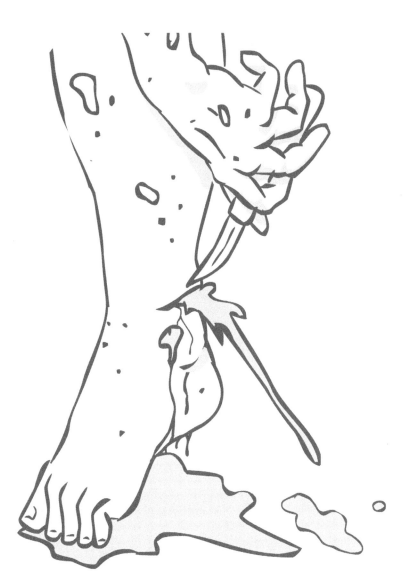

Release Pooling Blood By Cutting Leg.

How Smart Will I Be?
How Strong Will I Be?
Will "I" Be "Me" And Will I Be The Kind Of Bastard That Eats Families?

It depends, it depends, kind of, and yes you will!

While there are different types of Deads, we are all the kind of bastard that eats families. It's our nature. But cannibal is the wrong word. While, again, we do eat our own from time to time, we *feed* on Healthies. Healthies are a different species from what we have become all together. You are a Mortuus Sapien now, not a Homo Sapien. You are no longer human, and there is no going back. What exactly is a Mortuus Sapien you ask? Mortuus Sapien is Latin for "Wise" or "Knowing Dead". Homo Sapien on the other hand means "Wise" or "Knowing" Man. We are no longer men or women after we turn.

Homo Sapien

Main Entry: Homo Sa·pi·ens.
Pronunciation: Ho-mo Say-pee-enz
Function: Noun.
Etymology: New Latin, Homo + Sapiens, specific epithet, from Latin, "Wise Man". Definition: 1st extant species of the primate family Hominidae
Slang: Dudes, Chicks.

Mortuus Sapien

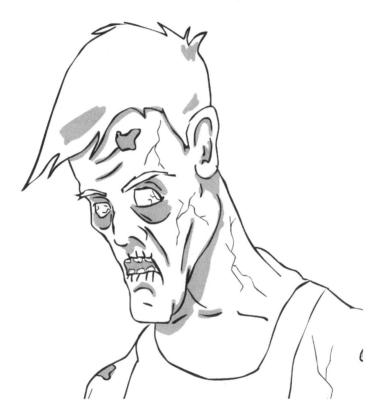

Main Entry: Mor·tuus Sa·pi·ens.
Pronunciation: Mor-tis Say-pee-enz.
Function: Noun.
Etymology: New Latin, Mortuus + Sapiens, specific epithet, from Latin, "Wise Dead". Definition: 2nd extant species of the primate family Hominidae (that includes Homo Sapiens) having human form and attributes and retaining some mobility and intelligence but clearly deceased. Feeds exclusively on the flesh and organs of Homo Sapiens.
Slang: Zombies, Ghouls, Deads.

So you see, "we" are not "them", so "you" will no longer be "you".

Now let's talk intelligence and mobility.

Now those of you reading this book that are alive are probably thinking "Zombie's can't read, much less publish books! This is ridiculous!" Good, keep thinking that and your kind will go down quickly. All of the valuable knowledge you've gained watching Hollywood's brilliant ideas of the Undead are surely correct, right? Wrong! First off, while I do have limited access to the necessary resources to write and publish a book, those that do I possess exist on a "Need to Know" basis. And, in my opinion, you don't really need to know. That information, as well as so much more, may quite possibly be made available in the future. We have our ways of getting things done, or should I say done for us. There is an unlimited supply of "help" available to our kind so that an invaluable book like this one can not only be written, but can be printed and widely distributed in order to help our kind thrive in this time of uncertainty.

The "Help"

It's safe to say that if you are reading a book published by a Dead then maybe the statements I am making about your turning being a "definite" should be taken seriously. Now the bit about Deads that can read. Movie "zombies" are just that, movie "zombies". There are many Classes of Deads and some of us are quite capable of almost anything. And we can have that ability naturally, or it can be attained through different means.

Some of you will have intelligence, but you won't seem to. This can range from human, to chimp, to dog, to cow, and to slug.

The highest Class of Deads, Class A of which I am a member, most certainly can read. And write. As can Class B, although at a lesser level. The following pages show a breakdown of the classification of Deads:

Class A. Sentient, nearly as advanced as we were in our lives before we turned.

While there are not a high percentage of us, maybe 1%, we do exist and can do or learn nearly everything we could do when we had to breathe. But don't get the idea we aren't dangerous. We are the most dangerous because we can teach the others how to hunt the living, or Healthies. One on one we can easily take the average Healthy. And we move smoothly and are pretty fast runners. Easily mistaken for Healthies from a distance, and we can speak.

Class B are more advanced than most, but in no way elegant. They can read simple things, as well as use and make tools effectively. Speech is slow and deliberate, but sometimes hard to understand. Locomotion is fairly quick, but you can tell Class B Deads are definitely not Healthies from any distance.

Class C are made up of those who can take direction and free think with limitations. They are followers mostly, but can hunt successfully. They also have limited communicative abilities. This group represents well over half of the Undead population.

Class D are shufflers but are aware and they "live". They are slow moving and scavenge for food mostly. With no desire to hide or stalk, these are the ones Healthies will see most often milling about streets and parks. And these are the ones they see us all as being like. It's good they don't know our full capabilities. Very good.

Class F are just what you think; Reactors, flesh sacks, "zombies". They don't last long and sometimes just sit and stare at the sun. They also pose little danger to Healthies.

What Exactly Are The Undead?

You are probably familiar with several types of the Undead, and monsters in general. Tales have been told from the dawn of time, most likely, of things that go "bump" in the night. Beings that are not alive, but not dead either. As humankind progressed these stories went from word of mouth to books and then ultimately to movies and television shows. Because of this, everyone thinks they have a firm grasp on all types of monsters and how they behave. But not everyone believes in them. True, many people believe in ghosts, but what about the other members of the Undead world? Interestingly enough most of the ones you are familiar with exist, but not necessarily in the Hollywood sense. They thrive and wage war against each other every day of their existence.

Let's examine some now.

Deads or "Zombies", yes. As I said, I refer to myself as a Dead and I hate the word "zombie". Deads have always been around throughout history, but never in as large an outbreak that is taking shape now.

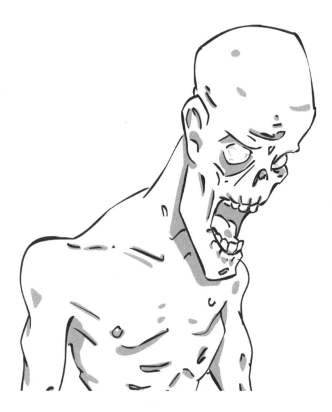

Dead ("Zombie")

Vampires, definitely. They are a constant, yet stealthy presence. They loathe Deads, as we eliminate their food supply exponentially. We kill Healthies, and create more who kill more Healthies. Vampires are the enemy.

Vampire

Werewolves. While I have never seen one, I have experienced evidence of their existence. More accurately categorized as a Monster as Werewolves are not truly "Undead".

Werewolf

Gill Men/Fish Men, doubtful but possible. They do not "start out" as human like the three above. They would be on their own branch of the evolutionary tree and hard evidence has never been found, which means nothing of course.

Gill Man/Fish Man

How Are Deads Created?

In fiction "Zombies" are created in many ways. The following is a list of some of them.

Radioactive Waste or other Bio-Hazardous Material left unchecked.

Radioactive Waste Drums

Satellites, Comets, Meteors, and other events coming to earth from outer space.

Comet/Meteor

And Viruses, among others.

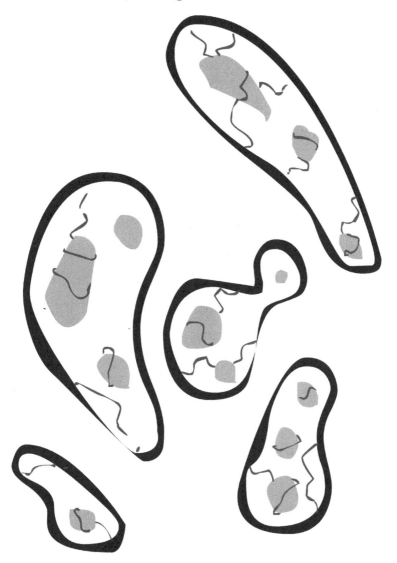

Viruses

Well, the latter turned out to be true it would seem. Along with a little wrath of an angry God. But the word wrath brings us back to viruses, and the cause. The virus that is causing this plague is called Wrath. It was designed specifically to be unleashed on an enemy to kill them, make their dead walk, and make those dead infect or feed on the living that remain.

A disease of Biblical proportion, the perfect weapon. A weapon designed to be used and then cured, by it's creators; The United States Department of Defense. But this isn't a lesson in the cause; this book's mission is to show you how to thrive. There is no reason to detail the cause because that will do no good at this stage of the game.

And yes it's a game, a game where responsibility for disaster lies in the hands of the last person you'd expect, your hands perhaps. The hands that fought more for the almighty dollar than for their neighbor. The hands that are still covered in the blood on innocents because of a lifestyle they could ill-afford without deceit. The hands you see everyday in front of you.

But if not for Wrath where would you be? Where would you have ended up?

Graveyard

Again, this isn't a lesson in the cause. Blame is a useless pursuit, and Time is the flame by which we all burn. Even the Undead...

What About A Cure?

Doctor And Infectee.

The possibilities for a cure, at least at this stage, are nil. Many experiments were done to produce a cure for this so-called plague that created us. And there was thought to be one for quite some time. Unfortunately it didn't work and Wrath ran rampant causing a global apocalyptic epidemic. So you see the cure that "was" is no more. There is absolutely no cure for this virus. There is no going back. If you have turned, you are a Dead. Period.

If you haven't turned, as I said before, you will. Prevention? Maybe temporarily Healthies can avoid their fates, but unless they plan on leaving the planet, their future is set. Think about it, no one gets out of here alive. We all die. It's going to happen. But now we don't stop being when we do. We walk on. It's that simple.

What To Do? Your Undead "To Do" List.

<u>Before you turn</u>- Be prepared. I understand and remember that the will of the Homo Sapien is strong, and if you haven't turned as yet you are probably thinking about how to survive this apocalypse and remain uninfected.

You may even have one of the many survival guides out there that tell you how to do it. But as we have discussed, the smart money is on you becoming one of us. So you might as well be ready. I have always gone by the assumption that your best defense is a good offense. Infecting yourself is fairly simple actually, and will leave you in better shape to thrive as a Dead. Many of us who have been turned incur injury in the process. Sometimes we are even partially eaten.

Doesn't it make sense to turn yourself and enter the realm of the Undead a fine physical specimen? I know I wrote earlier that merely dying will likely cause you to turn, but to be sure don't just kill yourself, infect yourself. This will guarantee you reanimate as a higher Class than you would have otherwise. The easiest way to accomplish this is to find a Dead, collect a sample of blood or saliva, and get it into your bloodstream.

A needle is not needed. The smallest cut is fine as the Wrath virus is extremely contagious. Even a small amount in the eye will do the trick. This can be done using a common eyedropper filled with infected bodily fluid. Sometimes even ingesting a small amount orally will do, but to be sure, and to make sure you don't waste the collected fluid, drop it into a cut or into your eye.

Drops Going In Eye

The point is a pristine body turned of your own free will yields a higher probability that you will be Class B or higher. Before you turn yourself, or if our boys and girls are beating on your door, at the very least put on a helmet; full face motorcycle is best but football or skateboard helmets will work as well.

This will keep you safe from simple head trauma that will threaten your undead existence after you turn. During transformation the "reanimation shock" can be daunting and leave you vulnerable. (More on reanimation shock later). While this usually doesn't last long, your vulnerability must be minimized. A skull protected with a helmet isn't vulnerable to blows from bats, golf clubs, bricks, etc. that a Healthy may rain upon you if you stumble upon them or they upon you. The length of reanimation shock may be long, or you may only get to Class C or D at first, so you need this protection while you wait for full cognizant animation. To protect the entire body, Kevlar enhanced motorcycle suits are excellent.

Protective Gear

Jacket and pants, as well as high quality boots and gloves, will help bolster your undead walking corpse.

This entire regalia will come in handy after you attain higher stages of reanimation as well. Think of it as your battle armor when taking on the uninfected Healthies. Simply put, you can and will thrive in the apocalypse if you do as I instruct. We will cover self-defense later in the Guide.

Some additional things to have on hand include raw meat. Meat from a large mammal is best. Beef will do, but ape, monkey, or any primate is better as it's closer to Homo Sapien. Have the meat in an obvious place so when you turn you can feed without running aimlessly and foolishly into the streets where waiting Healthies can eliminate you. The idea is control. Locking the door of your home, the best place to transform as I said, ensures that you will not be able to leave the home until you have gained enough intelligence to undo a lock.

Unlocking A Door

And again, you will. Movie "zombies" are just that, movies...

Now let's talk about better un-living through chemicals. Adrenalin, when injected into the Wrath infected body, enhances intelligence and physical ability. Methamphetamines are also effective. If possible I highly recommend you finding plenty of one or both of these and injecting yourself *before* you turn. And, if in any way possible, it would be a good idea to construct the laboratory equipment necessary to make Methamphetamines. They are nearly as effective as Adrenalin in magnifying the intellectual and physical ability of the Undead body. The problem is they need to be taken on a regular basis in most cases, so you will need to continue taking them in order to keep a higher level of cognizance. Following this with a cup of coffee will allow the caffeine to move the meth through your veins quickly.

If you are turning yourself, this is easy. If they are pounding on your door, it's best to be able to reach into your pocket or purse to retrieve the loaded hypodermic needle. Then, have ample amounts for after you turn. Keep it near the meat. Now there is a chance you will be Class B or above immediately, so leaving this book near the meat so you can begin reading immediately is also smart. And a pre-injection will almost guarantee Class B from the start.

<u>During the transformation-</u> "Reanimation Shock" is a highly traumatic experience in some cases.

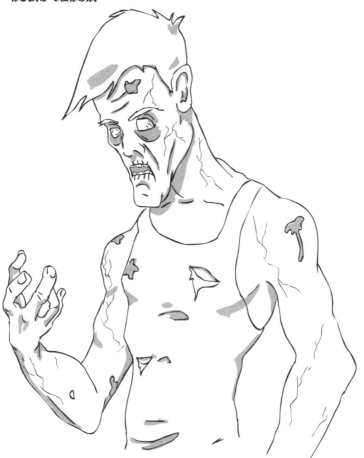

Reanimation Shock

Many of us forget it ever occurred afterwards, but handling it correctly is important. We discussed physical protection above but neglected to mention the prime location if one would decide to turn themselves. The best place is a quiet familiar place, your home. Lock the doors and transform in the comfort that comes from being surrounded by familiarity. Now, if you dislike your home, go somewhere calming. A favorite vacation spot, somewhere you used to live. The point is comfort. If you are turning yourself, Reanimation Shock (RS) will begin anywhere from a few minutes to a few hours after you infect yourself. During this time relax and let it happen. Convulsions will start as the virus takes your human life, and fluids will exit every orifice and pore. Severe vomiting is normal, as I said before.

You will die and soon come back. Placing yourself in front of a scene that makes you happy before you die will be calming as you reanimate, and as I said, will provide a better chance of a higher sentience as you progress.

Fear will be the most prevalent emotion. You will be scared, but it will pass. Replaced by blinding hunger that only one thing will satisfy...

After you turn- You will exit RS and the completion of your transformation will leave you hungrier than you have ever been, and just as anxious. You will be excited, confused, and the more time you wait to feed the more uncontrollable you will become. This is why you need the raw meat. You will be drawn to it and you will feed on it. The adrenalin and/or meth will hopefully be there as well as this book. The pre-shot of adrenalin and/or meth is important if intruders have eaten or destroyed your stockpiles you would have used later on.

One thing you need to expect is the possibility of Frenzy. Frenzy is a phenomenon caused by, among other things, close proximity of approximately 50 or more Deads for greater than 20 minutes.

Frenzy

This is an estimate given to me by a "friend" in one afterlife or another.

Frenzy causes us to attack each other uncontrollably, feeding on and killing our fellow Mortuus Sapiens.

It's uncontrollable and inescapable, so the only thing to do is let Darwinism work and do your best to prevail. Kill or be killed, cull the weak. Remember, however, that under normal circumstances the weak Class C and below Deads are still quite valuable. They will follow you and help win all battles against uninfected Healthies, so keep them close but not too close.

If you are in your home and safe, do not leave until you have read this entire Guide. You are going to need to know how to survive, and that includes knowing how to defend yourself from, and hunt, the living...

Healthies. The Enemy, And Your Food.

Healthies are a part of death. They are the enemy. They are our food. They are dangerous. Human beings, by nature, have a strong survival instinct. They will do anything to live. Think about it... Humans have no sharp fangs, claws, or animal strength. They don't even have fur to keep them warm. The only thing they have is their brain and their sheer will to survive, or more accurately, conquer. Most Deads, however, with the loss of all homeostasis are challenged with even the simplest of movement. This puts the Healthy at a considerable advantage. Too many times a Dead will shuffle right up to a Healthy completely oblivious as to whether he is armed with a weapon. Even the Class A and Bs may, when overly hungry, forget the rules and end up headless. What rules, you ask?

These...

1.   Never approach a Healthy from the front if the odds are less than five Deads to one Healthy. Their eyes, like ours, are close set and predatory. When desperate and given the chance, they will take the offensive and make short work of the average Dead. Class As should follow this rule out of principle.

2.   Attack from behind, preferably when Healthies have disrobed for sleep or sex. Many Healthies wear protective clothing and have weapons close at hand. But remember, when sleeping or having sexual intercourse they strip down and are at their most vulnerable.

3.   You can't outrun a bullet, but you don't have to reload a cricket bat (a simple, yet effective, Heatlhy favorite against Deads). A Healthy with a gun should NEVER be challenged. Just stay away. But a Healthy armed with a blunt instrument is also dangerous as this

weapon is an extension of the arm. Following Rules 1. and 2 closely will ensure an advantage.

4. Protect yourself with the proper gear, including a helmet and Kevlar plated clothing if possible. Also learn to use weapons. Don't attack as a "zombie", attack as a warrior.

Defending Yourself From The Living... "Healthies".

Defending yourself from the living is going to be a full time job. As we have covered, the weapons they could employ against you at any time include guns, knives, bats, and explosives.

Weapons

But unlike the "zombies" in film, YOU will be protected because YOU are not brainless!

First things first, protective gear. I discussed this earlier in the guide at least twice before because it's THAT important and so often overlooked. So I will mention it again, PROTECT YOUR HEAD, the Deads' Achilles Heel. And what better way than with a helmet designed to protect the head from trauma. A Motorcycle Helmet. If you didn't prepare before you turned and are unprotected, helmets shouldn't be too hard to find. Of course this won't be bullet proof, but it will stop most blunt or sharp instruments from penetrating your skull.

Tight Leather can hold a rotting body together, again motorcycle clothing comes to mind. However, many artificial materials or even heavy cotton clothing can help as well. Heavy gloves protect "finger attrition". This phenomenon is caused by the constant use of non-healing hands and fingers. Fingers will be torn off or skin and nails will rub off down to bone leaving you with stubs, eventually wearing down to the wrist.

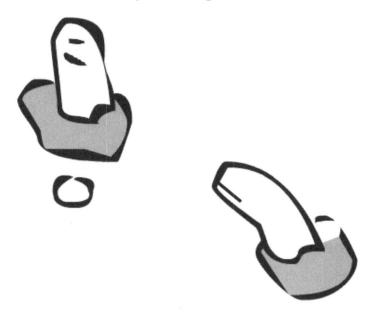

Detached Finger Tips

And on that note...

Repairs. Duct Tape is the Dead's best friend. Broken limbs, exposed cavities, and anything falling off can be held on with duct tape. And when the bones are the only thing at the end of your arms or hands, try sharpening them by rubbing them against cement or any other abrasive surface. This will turn old protruding bones into quite functional, and dangerous, weapons.

One thing Duct Tape cannot repair of course is burnt flesh, healthy or dead. Remember this: Flesh Good, Fire Bad. Under no circumstances should fire be used as a weapon as the physical limitations of most Classes of Dead are too great, making the chance of lighting oneself ablaze too great. The inability to adequately feel heat makes fire seem less dangerous and that is a hazard. Fire should be avoided at all costs.

Types Of Healthies.

There are many different types of Healthies. You will remember them all from your past life, and I have given some examples in the following pages. These, of course, are not all the types you will encounter, but they are a good sampling. In addition I give each a "Threat Rating" to let you know what to expect.

It's true that labeling humans negates them and can make them seem less dangerous.

This is definitely my objective here.

I am doing my best to educate you on how to survive and thrive in this apocalypse, and more importantly showing you how to effectively kill Healthies.

Survivalists
Threat Rating: 8/10

The Survivalist

Survivalists have been waiting for the apocalypse, however it would materialize. They lived for this, and they are prepared. The good thing is they are usually loners. The bad thing is they have all the supplies they need to survive and defend themselves, so it's not recommended you attack this type of Healthy alone. They may have fortified bunkers with thick walls and fences. Their weapons caches could include firearms, explosives, and booby traps set around the perimeter of their locales to eliminate any enemy, living or dead.

One of the worst adversaries is one who enjoys battle. Survivalists have sacrificed a lot to prepare for something that they most likely have been criticized for. They will have existed on the fringe of society for many years. Because of all of this they will receive a Threat Rating of 8/10, their biggest weakness being their habit of being loners.

Businessmen or Businesswomen
Threat Rating: 5/10

The Businessman

The Businessman or Businesswoman will be woefully unprepared for any type of apocalyptic event, and most will be killed or turned very quickly. They work and live near population centers and are usually weaponless. They may have a knife or handgun, but it's very doubtful. They will be soft from working at a desk, and the few gym workouts they do get will not afford them much in the way of endurance to avoid being caught. Their ability to organize may come into play, as well as their cut-throat nature. They will be a part of a large group and most likely sacrifice others to save themselves. This is not a bad thing, it means more easy food for you and your comrades.

Because of the relatively midrange threat these Healthies pose they receive a 5/10 Threat Rating. Stalk and attack at will, they will provide a well marbled meal.

Red Necks and Good Old Boys
Threat Rating: 7/10

The Redneck

The Red Neck, or the Good Old Boy. Historically joked about for their lack of intelligence, you may be fooled by memories creeping in from your former life. But be warned, the gun racks in their pickup trucks are for guns and this group of Healthies will have guns. Usually rifles and shotguns, as well as knives for close combat. They will combine the enjoyment of the battle of the Survivalist with the numbers of the Businessman. While not as prepared as the Survivalist, they will make up for it with large numbers and the ability to survive on less.

The Red Neck has a Threat Rating of 7/10. Beware, they have a strong sense of community and a willingness and ability to kill. Most hunt on a regular basis and you will be their prey if you allow this to happen.

Gangbangers
Threat Rating: 7/10

The Gangbanger

Gangbangers are very similar to Red Necks in their ability. They are an urban version of the Red Neck, but living largely in population centers they will be unable to last long. The larger the city, the quicker it will fall. The Undead spread where there are more people and this will cause Gangbangers to hole up in buildings in these cities. That means it's only a matter of time until they are killed and eaten. However until they are, they will be armed and ready to kill us, so they receive a Threat Rating of 7/10.

They will not last as long as water and food will be more scarce in the cities. This will cause them to expose themselves while trying to leave the city, and if they wait to long there will be too many of us to wade through. They will be nothing but a traveling smorgasbord.

Average Joe/Joan
Threat Rating: 6/10 – 10/10

The Average Joe

The Average Joe/Joan... The threat here is he could be, or have been, any of the other categories of Healthy we mention in this Guide. An Average Joe who was a soldier could now be a Survivalist in regular clothing. He could have been a Soldier, Cop, or Gangbanger, or could BE a Red Neck. He could even be a closet Geek. This is why you need to be very careful when confronting the Average Joe. He will only receive a Threat Rating of 6/10, but that rating could be as high as any of the other Healthies mentioned under the right conditions.

The Average Joe is the perfect bait to be used in a trap by a large number of Healthies. If you see one walking the streets, or in a field, unarmed and out in the open be wary. It could very well be a trap. When under attack an Average Joe can be more than you want to handle. Take if from an Average Joe turned Undead Monster.

Soldiers and Police
Threat Rating: 10/10 or 9/10

The Soldier

Soldiers... Need I say more? The most dangerous, and given a 10/10 Threat Rating. They will be armed and trained to kill any enemy. Rifle, Handgun, Knife, Grenade, C4, you name it and Soldiers have it. And their job is to defend.

The Police will be comparable to the Soldier, and nearly every bit as dangerous. But they are not usually as well armed; they receive a 9/10.

Both dangerous and trained to defend themselves and others, they should be avoided at all costs. Hide or run from this group. The good thing about them, however, is that they will be busy handling other Healthies who have become lawless. Martial Law will be in effect in the cities, suburbs, and rural areas and people being people there will be laws broken. While Soldiers and Police are occupied maintaining order among the Healthies, it will be easy for you to help tie up any loose ends so to speak.

Geeks (The Hidden Threat)
Threat Rating: 4/10 (9/10)

The Geek

Hidden Threat? You bet. Geeks seem easy to take down, but they know everything there is to know about us. Many guidebooks try and pretend that "zombie" defense techniques are completely unknown. This is just not true. Everyone knows to "shoot them in the head", but what about the other ways to eliminate us? A lot of Science goes into Science Fiction, and Geeks are steeped in this genre. They not only know exactly how to kill us, but the most efficient ways as well. For instance things as simple as fire, as complicated as high voltage electricity, and everything else in between are familiar to Geeks. In addition, they will most likely be releasing the kind of pent up rage that comes from being ostracized and poked fun at their entire lives. Their expert use of technology and communication make them a threat as well. For hand to hand Threat they get a 4/10, but for Threat to the Undead as a whole, they get a 9/10.

Soccer/Hockey Moms (and Dads)
Threat Rating: 3/10

The Soccer Mom

While it's fashionable to say how tough the so called Soccer/Hockey Mom (or Dad) is, they will go down as quick as the businessperson, if not quicker. The unfortunate truth is that someone who devotes their lives to their children's education and activities will not be prepared to defend themselves or their families in the time of a full-on apocalypse. They may also look like they are already members of the Undead population due to lack of sleep, but their screams will say different.

This type of Healthy will usually be found hiding with their families in their suburban homes. They will valiantly defend their brood to the death, making them an admirable adversary. Just not a challenging one. 3/10 Threat Rating here, enjoy your meal...

Small Children and The Elderly
Threat Rating: N/A – 2/10

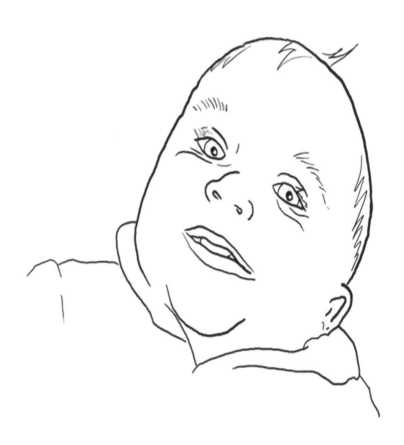

The Small Child

Nothing else really needs to be said. This is WAR against the Healthies, and young Healthies become ADULT Healthies that want us gone from the face of the earth. So eliminating them is not only an easy meal, but a service to our kind. Having said that, they are children and the emotional aspect of killing and eating a child could cause undo emotional trauma in the higher Classes of Deads. But this will only be temporary. If you do find yourself in close quarters with a young Healthy the urge to feed will be strong. Like a drug, Wrath owns you, and you will most likely engage, however cruel that may sound.

The elderly are also an easy mark but will most likely die quickly in the time of apocalypse. Those that survive will also be an easy meal, quite frankly.

Neither of these are much of a threat, but the elderly may be armed, earning them a 2/10.

Stalking & Killing Techniques.

The one main advantage you have over ALL Healthies is simply this. You were once them, they were never you. While stalking techniques will need to be modified based on the individual type of Healthy mentioned above, there are a few general things you need to keep in mind. Blindly staggering toward a group of Healthies is fine for Class Ds and Fs. They have to rely on their numbers to successfully attack and feed. But Cs and above, we need to work together and hunt smart.

Detecting Healthies is something that may not come to you immediately, but it will come. First, your sense of smell, and taste, will be heightened. Open your mouth wide and draw air in through your nose and mouth. You will be able to smell *and taste* Healthy flesh from a mile away. It smells sweet, almost like a flower, and even sweeter when the flesh is full of fear.

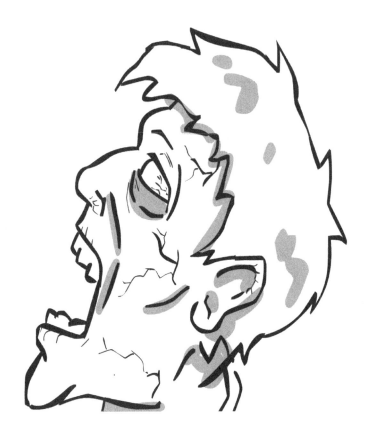

Smell And Taste Healthies From Afar.

This combination of flesh and fear will act on your undead brain like nothing you have ever felt. The compulsion to shred someone apart will burn inside you brewing a hunger, a primal urging, to kill and feed upon the flesh of the living.

Sight will be limited in many of us, and hearing will be good, but confusing at times as we try to decipher different sounds and speech. Scent is how we hunt, and it's most effective.

Healthies, all of them, are at their weakest and most vulnerable during sex and sleep, as we covered before. And you can smell them as easily at night as during the day. This is why nocturnal attacks are the most successful ones.

When Healthies are coupling their minds are on one thing and it's not protecting themselves from attacks by the Undead. This lapse in awareness is what we must exploit. Hearing is not as in tune and they will not be visually alert, especially if it's dark. And when undressed, Healthies are usually at their weakest.

Unaware Healthies.

And as far as sleep goes, be as quiet as you can and you will feed easily. They have to sleep. We don't have to, but we sometimes will. This is yet another of our advantages.

Once you are upon your prey what is the best way to kill and eat them? If you have a weapon, the most successful kill will come from its proper use. Shooting a Healthy in the heart or head will kill them, and shooting them almost anywhere will weaken them to the point of an easy meal. Blunt objects to the head are also effective, but using a complicated weapon like a gun is better for two reasons:

First, of course, using a gun is much more effective and you can kill from a distance.

Second, and my personal favorite really, is that most Healthies stubbornly hold on to the belief that Deads are non-intelligent flesh sacks that can't use even the crudest of tools. Whether they believe this out of laziness or because it makes them feel safe and in control is no matter.

As I covered before, most of us, even the Class Ds to an extent, can learn, just at a slower rate. We have the ability to do many things. The truth is we are smarter than they think.

Dead Aiming A Firearm.

So if there are weapons available use them and teach others. If you don't know how, find someone in your group that has used them and have them instruct those that have not. Also, force human captives to teach you.

Don't forget how this book was produced.

Penetrating Personal Defenses.

While many Healthies will be in "street clothes" some will have armored themselves as you have been instructed to do. This will necessitate the use of weapons by YOU. As we said above, and this is worth repeating, most Deads know or can learn nearly everything. It's not unusual for Class C Deads to become fairly adept with close-quarters weaponry like knives and clubs.

If there are no weapons to be found remember this; You can't bite through Kevlar so look for skin and cloth. The average Healthy will have donned any protective clothing he is wearing in haste and there will be holes. Tear at the clothing, as quite often you can remove what you can't bite through. It's imperative that you never stop the attack. Be tenacious, be vigilant, and you will feed.

Feeding.

There's really not much to say here. When it comes to feeding, I like to eat the Healthy while it's still alive. I start with the face and watch the horror build and listen to the music in their screams. This, along with the meal, makes me feel a great sense of peace. I highly recommend, however, that you wait until you are a skilled hunter of Healthies before you take this approach. For now, kill them quickly to protect yourself and your group. This will keep you strong and teach you about stalking and killing them.

Art by Alan R. Gandy

Places To Hunt.

We've covered how to stalk, kill, and feed but where do you hunt Healthies? Where do you find them? You must simply look wherever large groups of them will gather in the time of uncertainty and apocalypse. Hospitals, schools, office buildings, churches, even bars. Smell, watch, and listen for clues, they will be there. Look for lights at night. Smell for fear. Listen for any kind of speech or the sounds of machinery.

But beware of Military bases. Stay away from these unless you have an army of your own (more on this later) as they will likely be home to experiments and other atrocities done on our kind.

Compromising places of residence has been portrayed in film as a difficult task. Everyone seems to have an unlimited supply of boards and nails, not to mention tools, to keep us out. This usually isn't the case. A simple door is sometimes all that stands in the way of you and your meal.

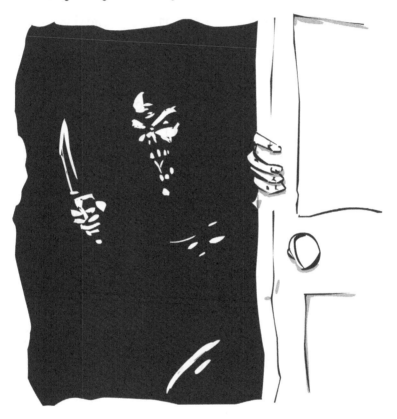

Knife-Wielding Dead Entering A Residence.

If the entrance is locked or barricaded, use something in the environment around you to smash windows and doors. In film, again, it's always an arm coming in the window blindly. How Neanderthal. Remember WEAPONS. Use a club, bat, knife, or gun. Think like a soldier, because that is what you are. We are at WAR with the Healthies and need to treat the situation as such.

Everyone Needs A Home.

We've talked about how to hunt, who to hunt, and when to hunt... But where are you going to "live"?

Dead At Home.

Everyone needs a home and so do the Undead. The City is truly a "Zombie Wonderland", at least at first. There will be plenty of food for quite a while, and more Deads than Healthies. But when the Healthies strike back, the cities are where they will strike to get rid of as many of us as they can. True, this could take quite a while, and depend on many different factors, but it needs to be considered. When in the city, Frenzy will occur given the large amounts of Deads. This is one of our biggest weaknesses and some Healthies know this. And it's another reason to head for more open spaces within the city, and not congregate too much in one space.

Taking over buildings and eradicating the Healthies within will be a challenge, but the ones that hide are usually the easiest to kill. A new Dead Society is not too far out of reach at any given time.

Islands seem like a good choice, but many will have been turned into Healthy strongholds. The prevailing idea here is that Healthies can kill all of us on an island and then be safe because we can't get to them. This is very wrong, but the Healthies will be watching the shores, if not for us for dangerous Healthies. Therefore island living is not the smartest bet.

The suburbs may seem like only a great place to raid and feed, but bad for a home. This is not necessarily so. Healthies will have fled the suburbs for the most part to head for "high ground", leaving the area to a few pockets of them. This makes for some food and a fairly stable place to be.

The forest and rural areas are a bad idea at first, but a good place to hide if the Healthies start a comeback. This will simply be an existence of wandering aimlessly, but survival is key.

In short, it's wisest to remain near the population centers until it's no longer feasible to stay there...

Animals.

As far as animals other than humans are concerned, the question often arises as to whether or not they will turn. The answer is simple. Some may turn, others won't. All have the ability to turn. Animals that turn seem to be in a constant state of a sort of Frenzy. They are usually ready to attack, but mostly only Healthies, human and animal. For the most part they leave us alone, except for infected canines.

Healthy animals are a different story...

Dogs are one of our biggest enemies in the animal kingdom. Wild animals will attack us, but are usually scared of us as they are scared of Healthy humans. Dogs, however, view us as the enemy and are not afraid. They are used by Healthies to attack and control us. To tear us apart, and even to spread diseases and viruses only we can catch. They are a fairly effective weapon

locally, but as a weapon to wipe us all out
not as much. Infected dogs are even more
dangerous. They attack us with the same
ferocity as a healthy animal, but are nearly
unstoppable.

Infected Dog

Stay away from dogs, infected or healthy,
no matter how friendly they may seem at
first.

Maggots and other parasites usually don't effect us too much, as the Wrath virus kills and infects them if they feed on us. Smaller bugs like this usually don't survive the infection.

This is not to say there will never be times you hear them scratching inside your skull as they begin to feed on your brain. The sound can get quite intense, but it doesn't last long as they will soon die from the effects of Wrath. Frankly if Wrath didn't kill these organisms we could not survive.

Weather And Temperature.

An important part of our survival is to maintain the proper temperature. Cold climates are not conducive to the survival of the Undead.

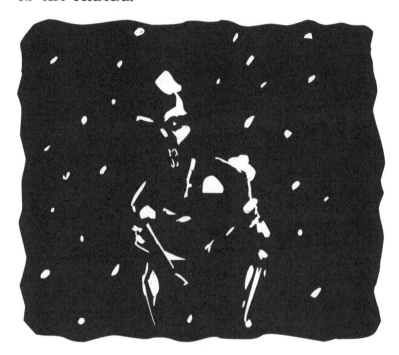

Cold Is The Enemy.

Plain and simple, the lower Classes, C and below, do not fair well as they do not think of staying warm. For the most part they don't feel cold and just freeze up if not protected by enough clothing. Even Class A and B Deads need to constantly remember to stay warm or joints and muscles will freeze and leave us immobile in the cold. Healthies retreat to these regions to hide, as well they should, but so many don't realize that some of us are intelligent enough to dress for the cold. Attacks in the North are usually not defended as they are unexpected.

Terrain can be challenging as well. Rotting limbs are full of rotting muscles and ligaments that do not fair well with use. There is not healing in most of us, unless we are altered genetically in some way or heavily on Adrenalin or Meth. Even then our bodies deteriorate at a faster level than Healthies. Hard terrain and mountainous regions will take their toll and missteps can lead to lost limbs.

Raise An Army.

...or join one. Much of this book is a thinly veiled attempt to get you to become a soldier in the war against Healthies. They are killing us, experimenting on us, and leaving us to die. And it's going to get worse before it gets better. We must organize and eliminate them for our own survival. They have to die and suffer at the hands of OUR Armies as we have at the hands of theirs. We are angry, we are ready, and many of us are intelligent.

Think of defeating the Healthies as a way to inner peace. Deads will never rest in peace until all Healthies are dead and gone. Maybe this is why we exist. To eliminate Homo Sapiens as the Alpha Predator and replace them entirely.

It has become quite clear that the time of Homo Sapiens has past.

And the time of Mortuus Sapiens has only just begun...

We Are Many...

The End

.

CPSIA information can be obtained at www.ICGtesting.com
Printed in the USA
LVOW01s1448251013

358633LV00011B/543/P